FICTION IN A FLASH!
SIX TALES OF TERROR

Based on

Flash Fiction Shorts

By

T.K. Millin

Fiction in a Flash! Six Tales of Terror

Efi Loo Publishing, Inc.

efiloopublishing@gmail.com

First paperback edition.

ISBN-13: 978-0615798172

ASIN: B00BFCHZ1Y (EBook)

Cover Design Copyright © Efi Loo Publishing, Inc., 2013

EFI LOO PUBLISHING

DEDICATION

Each of these stories is dedicated to the works of Madeleine L'Engle, Edgar Rice Burroughs and Edgar Allan Poe. Their imaginary worlds captivated me in my youth and continue to inspire me today as a writer.

To my husband, your constant belief and support inspires me to venture out and grow as a writer.

CONTENTS

FORWARD

A little backstory about the tales you are about to read.

Welcome to the world of flash fiction! Flash fiction was started by different communities of writers from all genres, who set out to challenge, and inspire, one another to write a short story (usually between 500 and 1,500 words) each week based on a different theme. This platform provided authors the opportunity to keep their creative juices flowing and to have their work read and critiqued by other writers. After each flash heading, you will find the theme the story was based on.

Thank you for your interest in Fiction in a Flash! It is my desire this collection of six tales (plus the added bonus tale not found in the EBook version!) takes you somewhere far, far, away; even if only for the very short time it will take you to read them.

T.K. Millin

Flash One – The Other Side of Here
Based on the theme: Hell

The purple sands of the planet dubbed, LBX One Nine, swirled around the spacecraft as it descended on the jagged peaks of the undiscovered world. The hatch doors swung open and all five crewmembers of Deep Space Voyager descended down the ramp and into the darkened landscape they'd only seen through the eye of a telescope ten million light years away; ten million light years from the day before yesterday.

"Holy Bejeezus!" Commander Blake dropped to his knees and clutched a glove full of sand. "I was convinced Professor Finklestein had sent us off to our deaths with his black hole theory." He opened his grip and watched the purple sand whirl into the darkness. "Where's Flight Engineer Huntley?" He asked, seeing only three of his crew.

"He was here a second ago." Crew Chief Jackson looked behind him. "Knowing Huntley, he probably went back inside the ship so his shield wouldn't mess up his hair."

The Commander ordered Jackson to go and advise Huntley the two of them were to split up and search the surrounding landscape while he and Mission Specialist Ritter and Doc Wilson did the same.

Jackson stomped up the ramp. "Always giving orders, but never following them. That'll all change when I'm in charge."

Ritter reached out her hand. "Let me help you, Commander." She grabbed him by the wrist and lifted him up from his knees, pulling off his communications pad.

"Thanks, Ella."

Wilson picked up the pad and handed it to the Commander. "Being the only woman on board doesn't stop her from taking control."

1

Ritter snatched it from his hand. "I'm in control, remember, Doc?" She winked, blowing him a kiss.

The Commander stretched out his arm. "And, I'm in charge. Now, reconnect my communications pad and spread out." They turned their face shields to night vision and synchronized their GPS'.

The six red moons, glowing like fireballs against the black void of LBX One Nine's horizon, should have been a warning to the three as they each ventured into the barren landscape, alone.

＊＊＊＊

Flight Engineer Huntley opened his eyes and sat up. "Where am I and why is it so damn dark?" He engaged his suit's emergency light. "How the hell did I get inside a cave?" He touched the back of his throbbing head and slowly moved his blood-drenched hand into the beam. "Where's my shield?"

Following the direction of dripping water Huntley wandered into the darkness, his emergency light barely leading the way. Becoming disoriented with each twist and turn he stopped to check his GPS. "Damn it." He turned on his communications pad. "Hello, Commander, come in." He slammed his fist against the blank screen. "Somebody come in, damn it!" Echoes of clattering approached him from behind. "Thank, God. They found me." Relieved, he turned toward the encroaching vibrations.

A rush of panic overcame Flight Engineer Huntley as he realized there would be no rescue, only death from the gnawing and gnashing of teeth.

＊＊＊＊

"Doc, I've found something!" Ritter shined her beam of light across the reflecting surface. "And, it's beautiful."

He tracked her on his GPS. "Don't do anything, Ella. I'm there in two seconds!" Walking up beside her, he added his beam of light to hers. "It's a lake."

"I know, isn't it amazing?"

"Do you know what this means, Ella?"

"I know what it could mean." She ran her gloved hand up and down the front of his suit.

"No, it means there could be life here. It also means there's oxygen." He lifted his shield and took in a deep breath of the sweet tasting air.

"It also means we're ten million light years away from our spouses." She lifted her shield and undressed. "It's perfect!" She said, wading deeper into the lake.

The reflection of her delicious curves reflecting off the water's ripples drove him to the point of no return. Without hesitation, or thought of regret, he joined her with every inch of his pulsating desire.

"We better get out, Ella, and suit up before the Commander finds us like this." His warm breath blew across her lips.

"He'll never know. I've made sure of it."

"What do you mean?"

She smirked. "Remember when the Commander's communications pad fell off his wrist and I put it back on?"

"Yeah."

"Well, I turned off the volume."

"You mean he can't hear us?"

She nodded.

"Oh, I do love your devilish ways." He took her by the waist and pulled her tight against his.

"Doc, you are making me so hot."

"No, it's you who is making me hot."

Suddenly the lake erupted into flames, consuming Mission Specialist Ritter and Doc Wilson in their sinful embrace.

* * * *

Commander Blake knew he had broken the code of survival when he ordered his crew to spread out without being in pairs. He now found himself the same victim he had always preached against to his underlings.

"Ritter, Huntley, Wilson, Jackson, come in!" He pounded on his communications pad. "Damn it, where are they?"

A faint blinking light appeared on his GPS. "Jackson?" He followed the signal back to Deep Space Voyager and, on seeing the darkened ship, paused before ascending the ramp.

He shined his emergency light around the control room. "Holy Bejeezus!" Jackson hung upside down, worms devouring the remaining flesh from his half-eaten torso.

"My apologies, but Jesus can't hear you here." The enraged voice said.

Commander Blake spun from side to side. "Who's there?" Getting no response, he added. "As the Commander of Deep Space Voyager, I demand you show yourself!"

A towering shadow glided out from behind the central control station. Commander Blake fluttered the beam of light up and down the figure. "Father?"

"You can call me Father, if you like." The warm gentle smile on Commander Blake's belated father's face turned to a raging ball of fire. "But I prefer Lucifer."

"Oh my God, we all died when we traveled ten million light years into space and now we're in Hell!"

"No. You all were very much alive when you arrived here and my minions and lake of fire have been waiting since the dawn of creation to feast on live flesh."

"God, please, help me!"

"There's no need to cry out for your God. He can't help you here. When you crossed over from the other side you broke the rules. You are in my world now, and I choose who lives and who dies. And I choose for you to live forever!"

"And they will go out and look upon the dead bodies of those who rebelled against me; their worm will not die, nor will their fire be quenched, and they will be loathsome to all man."

Isaiah 66:24

Flash Two – The Forbidden Treehouse
Based on the theme: Evil Spirit

The overstuffed room with its reminiscing scent of stale wet bread and cigarettes long ago puffed dry made me feel at home. My right thumb swirled around the inside of my left palm as I sat listening to the sobbing woman, praying when it was my turn everyone would believe me, too.

The AA counselor's faded green eyes glistened off the scorching overhead light the size of a Mack truck. "Thank you, Maryann, for again sharing with us your story on becoming an alcoholic. Everyone, please join me in giving Maryann another round of applause." She searched the cramped room. "Now, it's time we heard from someone new." Making direct eye contact with my avoiding eyes, she said, "How about you there in the back corner, we'd love to hear your story."

I checked the room from side to side for the familiar face that haunted me, but found only the blank stares of weary eyed strangers. I released the pressure of my thumb from my palm and made my way toward the front of the room, as if I had all the time in the world.

The counselor stood and scraped her chair off to the side. "Please, start by telling us your name."

"Um, hi, my name is Tom. Um, Tom Stanton." I reached into my worn overcoat pocket and squeezed my only comfort, a fifth of whisky. "I'm an alcoholic and I'm haunted by an evil spirit."

The overflowing room of mirrored images of depression echoed with whispers and undertones of laughter. The counselor cleared her throat. "Please, let Tom tell his story."

I released my hold on the whisky bottle and took a deep breath. "Um, it all began more than thirty years ago. It was the middle of August, which always seemed to be the hottest month of the year growing up in Louisiana.

It always made summer vacations feel like they dragged on forever for my three best friends and me. Clayton Moore, Jerry Malone and Maggie Devereaux, each of us only months away from our sixteenth birthday."

I paused and licked my lips; gulping down what saliva I could muster. "A day never passed that the four of us couldn't be found exploring the surrounding swamps for slithering critters, dried up crawfish or burned out campfires from drunken gator hunters telling tall tales the night before. It was the morning of August 16, 1972 and it would have been like any other morning out on the bayou, if it hadn't been for our discovery." My memory wandered back to the day that changed my life forever . . .

* * * *

"Hey, guys, hurry up. Look what I found." Jerry shouted in the distance.

Maggie rolled her eyes. "Great, I suppose he found another snake with its head chopped off."

Clayton nodded. "We better go and see what he's found before he does something stupid." I agreed and the three of us went in search of Jerry's discovery, discussing how today was just as boring as yesterday.

Coming around a bend, Jerry stood staring up at the sky. His jaw hung open as if catching flies.

Curious, I joined him in his fascination. "Wow, would you look at that!" The naked branches of a giant cypress tree curled and twisted toward the clouds. At the very tip of their boney-like fingers sat a small wooden house with a rope ladder dangling from a window all the way down to the ground.

Jerry grabbed the ladder with both hands. "I'm going up. You all stay here!"

I looked at Maggie and Clayton. "We go together or not at all."

Clayton smiled. "You can count me in."

Maggie nodded. "Okay, but I'm not going last."

Jerry climbed up the ladder at lightning speed. Clayton went next and I agreed to go last, for Maggie's sake. "Push, Tom. Push!" Maggie ordered while Clayton pulled her by the arms. "Oh, I'm too fat!"

"You'll fit." I firmly pressed the palms of my hands against each of her sweaty butt cheeks. "On the count of three. One. Two. Three!" Maggie flew through the window, followed by a crash and a thump.

I dragged myself inside. Maggie and Clayton were rolling around on the floor, laughing. Jerry sat at a rickety table in the corner. "Quit fooling around you all and come over here and check out what I found."

I walked up behind Jerry first, followed my Maggie and then Clayton. Jerry swept the dust-covered book with his hands, blowing off the remainder. A strange face carved out of a piece of dried wood stared back at us. "Wow!" Jerry opened the cover and turned the yellowed pages. Reaching the last page, he stuttered the words, "H-e…w-h-o…"

I grabbed the book from his hands. "Let me read it. We don't have all day." I read aloud the only words on the page.

Jerry punched Clayton on the right arm. "You don't believe that phony baloney stuff do you?"

Clayton returned the punch. "Nah, that's just some silly book put here to go along with that stupid made up legend of the forbidden treehouse meant to keep us kids out of the bayou."

Maggie laughed. "Ooh, I'm so scared."

The treehouse violently swayed from side to side and the sun disappeared like magic, and through the blackened silence Maggie, Jerry and Clayton's screams rang throughout the bayou.

* * * *

Without hesitation I pulled the bottle from my pocket, turned the cap and guzzled. "After all these years I still can't bring myself to repeat the words I read in that book."

The counselor moved her chair next to mine and sat and crossed her legs. "Tom, I think it would help if you gave it a try. You'll see. Everything will be alright." The room nodded in agreement.

I searched the room from side to side, and sighed. "Okay. Here goes nothing." I raised the bottle above my head, as a toast, and then guzzled it dry. "He who should speak these last words from my dying breath shall forever be haunted by me, the spirit of the forbidden treehouse. He who should not believe in me shall reap the wrath of my fury upon their flesh."

The counselor pulled a tissue from her pocket and dabbed her eyes. "I must say, Tom Stanton, you had me going there for a minute."

"But, it's all true. I really am being haunted."

One by one the weary-eyed strangers' blank stares and the counselor's smile turned to gut wrenching laughter. And, as if magic, the room turned to midnight and the earth rumbled beneath my feet, turning their roaring laughter into bone chilling screams.

The overstuffed room with its reminiscing scent of stale wet bread and cigarettes long ago puffed dry soon became a reminder to me that I will forever be haunted by the spirit of the forbidden treehouse.

Flash Three – Abandoned
Based on the theme: Little Shop of Oddities

The speedometer teetered between fifty and fifty-five as the 1974 Gremlin made its way down the lone highway toward the setting sun. Cassidy reached out with her right hand and turned up the radio volume as high as it would go. "Seasons in the Sun, my favorite!" She flicked through the overflowing ashtray and pulled out the tiny remnants of the Columbian Gold she had spent half of last week's pay on and pushed in the lighter, bouncing her head from side to side while singing along in unison.

The Gremlin spat and sputtered to a slow grind. "Damn it!" Cassidy tapped the gas gage. With the last of the engine's momentum, she swerved onto the right shoulder and pulled out the lighter and pressed its glowing tip against the singed joint. "Thank, God!"

Cassidy's state of self-induced euphoria vanished with the engulfing thickness of night. Searching for hours through the endless dark, she soon realized her only hope for help was in the rising sun.

* * * *

Waking to crunching footsteps and a flickering light, Cassidy sat up and rolled down the window. "Man, I never thought I'd be so happy to see a cop."

"Ya alright, Miss?" He said, shining the flashlight in her face.

Cassidy blocked the glare with her left hand. "Yes, Sir, my car ran out of…" Frogs serenaded to the beat of her heart.

The gangly stranger bent forward into the light. "Why I's just live up the road a piece. Be'd happy to give ya a ride." He lifted his hat and proudly displayed his lack of dental hygiene.

"I… I think I'll just wait until a policeman comes along."

"Reckon you'd be waiting a long time." Cassidy's stomach rumbled over the creaking and quacking of the frogs. He moved the beam of light up and down her torso. "My mama's making a big pot of stew with lots of chunks of juicy beef and potatoes. If ya hungry."

Cassidy pressed her hand against her stomach to muffle the next wave. "Well, I suppose if your Mother is going through all the trouble."

The over used pickup sped down the highway, squeaking with every dip in the road. Without slowing, the truck took a sudden turn left and the only working headlight flashed across a freshly painted sign. "You're name is Mr. Strange?" Cassidy reached for the door handle.

He threw his head back, breaking into ear-piercing laughter. The truck bounced down the zigzagging path as the words from the freshly painted sign flashed through Cassidy's horrified mind. *Mr. Strange's Little Shop of Weird.*

Frantically searching for a door handle, Cassidy realized the only hope she had was that her death would be quick and painless.

* * * *

The vibration of the hybrid engine blended with the surrounding silence of the lone highway as Jeremy drove toward the rising sun. He reached with his right hand and adjusted the angle of the GPS, when his phone rang. He pushed the hands free option on the steering wheel. "Ironside Realty."

"Hey, Jeremy, heard you were coming back into town! Wanna party tonight?"

"No, Dale. I'm only here on business. You know how I feel about this place ever since my sister's disappearance."

"Yeah, man, I know. I just thought..." The connection turned to static.

"Hello, Dale, are you there?" Jeremy tapped the steering wheel and then the GPS. "Shit, I lost all signals." Familiar with the unchanged landscape, Jeremy drove straight toward the glaring sun with only his memory as a guide.

Bored, he pulled down the visor and randomly selected a CD. "Hum, Hits of the 70's, why not." He slid the disk into the player and clicked the volume button on the underside of the steering wheel three times. "Seasons in the Sun. Please, anything but that!" Jeremy punched the seek button several times. "Now that's what I'm talking about." Turning the volume up two notches, he nodded side to side to the beat of 'Sundown'.

Three songs later and two bags of chips, washed down by a warm soda, Jeremy arrived at what he believed to be his destination. A tall tower of overgrown vines fluttered in the breeze. Out of nowhere came a gust of wind, blowing them apart. "Mr. Strange's Little Shop of Weird. Hum, not the place I was looking for." He checked his watch. "Oh, why not, I have time to spare." With his curiosity peaked, Jeremy followed the twists and turns along the dusty path until the very end.

He pulled onto the overgrown yard of dandelions and turned off the ignition. Dry rotted shutters dangled from the window frames of the unpainted wooden house. Storms had blown all but a row of moldy shingles off the roof and every grime-covered window had been smashed. The only thing untouched by time was a sign swinging over the dilapidated front porch, welcoming visitors to Mr. Strange's Little Shop of Weird.

Jeremy hesitated before maneuvering his way up the disintegrated steps. "This should be interesting." He pushed his way through the remaining slats used to make the front door and stepped inside. "Hello, is anyone here?"

The small unkempt room was stuffed with strange creatures made from road kill. A two-headed rabbit sat atop a deer turned unicorn. An armadillo with eight legs stood next to a dog with a rattlesnake tail and a bobcat with a chicken beak pecked away at a barrel of fake corn.

Jeremy cringed. "Okay, that's a little weird."

He crept his way down an unlit hallway, searching for a light switch. "Hello, is there anybody here?" Stepping into the ramshackled kitchen, he pinched his nose. "What in the world is that smell?" Eager to explore, he continued down the darkened hallway.

Peering inside the bathroom, Jeremy gulped back the reemerging taste of his breakfast. "Dear, God. That explains it!" Faded wallpaper of smiling chickadees drooped in long shredded strands. A sink encrusted in rust barely hung on the wall below a blackened cracked mirror. A toilet overflowing with red-brown slime, covered with swarming flies, stood next to an empty sand pit.

Making his way to the end of the hallway, he paused in front of a closed door, and tried the handle. "Oh, why not, it's obvious no one lives here." He slammed his shoulder against the door. "Crap that hurt." Standing back, he kicked open the aging wood.

Strange figures made of sewn together body parts from animals and humans crowded the room. A German shepherd with a human torso lifted its left leg on a skunk with human eyes and teeth. A turtle with human hands touched the paws of a grotesque half-bear, half-human creation. Jeremy tilted his head and walked up to the strange oddity, touching its decomposed face. "Oh, my God, Cassidy!" Cupping his hand over his mouth, Jeremy hoped he'd make it to the bath from hell in time.

"I's never did know her name." Mr. Strange raised the hatchet above Jeremy's head.

Jeremy spun and heaved across Mr. Strange's boots. Slipping and sliding, Mr. Strange struggled to gain his balance as he fell backwards onto the newly sharpened hatchet.

Realizing what he had to do, Jeremy ripped the hatchet from Mr. Strange's spine and, with all his might, swung it through the half-bear, half-human's neck. "Time for you to come home, Cassidy."

Flash Four – The Keeper
Based on the theme: Haunted Lighthouses

The harrowing winds swirled upward from the relentless waves as they crashed the last of their journey against the towering cliffs. The red and white lighthouse stood unwavering in the chill of the night, its twirling beacon of light a reminder to the passing ships on the horizon that danger lurked in the distance.

William Young tossed and turned beneath the crumpled sheets, as if running from the whispering voice. "You shall never forget." Bolting upright, he clutched his chest and gasped for relief.

Elizabeth mumbled. Stirring, she sat up and softly slid her hand across his golden beard. "William, please tell me what is troubling you."

"Nothing is of trouble my darling." He brushed her hand aside.

"But, William, night after night you awaken in sweat."

He stood and stretched, popping a button off the worn long johns he outgrew months ago. "I must go and refill the lighthouse lamp." Shivering, he dressed into a pair of overalls, pulled on his fisherman boots and grabbed his tattered wool coat, cap and gloves. "Please, go back to sleep." He bent down and kissed her forehead, squeezing his eyes shut at the touch of her frigid skin.

William turned up the brass lamp's flame and silently made his way through the one room cabin, casting dancing shadows in his wake. Inch by inch, he opened the door he promised Elizabeth he'd oil back in September and stomped across the frozen lawn.

November was his least favorite month being the head keeper of the Twin Rock Lighthouse, because he knew how unforgiving Lake Superior could be. He also knew that's why tonight would be the perfect night to carry out his plan.

Step by step he climbed the spiraling staircase, replaying inside his head the whispering voice that had been haunting him for months. "It must be my imagination playing tricks with me. I've made sure not a soul suspects a thing." Tiny slivers of ice crystals clung to the ends of his beard.

Stuffing the furnace pot with coal, he sat and warmed his hands by the flames and waited for the foghorn to blast its midnight announcement. The smashing of the waves washed away the anguish in William's heart, flooding it with memories of happier times when he and Elizabeth were first married.

Suddenly, the spiral staircase echoed in pounding footsteps . . .

* * * *

"Everyone step inside, there's plenty of room." The tour guide helped the eager crowd step through the small doorway. "Alright, watch ya step."

Little Jimmy ran to the north port window and stepped up on a wooden box below. "Wow, you can see forever from here!"

"You betcha." The tour guide grinned. "Why that's the same window William Young, the original keeper, watched and waited for the Elizabeth Dame." He pointed to a faded black and white photo on the wall. The crowd turned and stretched their necks to get a glimpse of the smiling man standing in front of a magnificent clipper ship.

Little Jimmy jumped from the box and ran to his father, stretching up his arms to be lifted. "So what's the big deal about that old ship?"

"Ya, a good question." The tour guide cleared his throat. "What's ya name, young lad?"

"Jimmy Taggert!"

"Well, Jimmy Taggert, that old ship happened to be one of the deadliest shipwrecks the Twin Rock Lighthouse has ever had. But the worst part is, it was all carefully planned." A hush fell over the room.

Having the crowd's full attention, the tour guide continued . . .

"It happened on one of the coldest and stormiest nights on record for these parts. It was November 21, 1910 and back in those days the lighthouse lantern had to be refueled every few hours with kerosene, so as he did every night, William Young climbed the spiral staircase to perform his nightly keeper duties. Only on that night he intentionally didn't do his keeper duties, for that night he had planned to commit murder."

"Murder!"

"You betcha, Jimmy. It's told by the locals here that William Young waited months to carry out his plan, because he knew by mid November you could count on there being a storm on Lake Superior almost every night. That night his waiting paid off for a ferocious storm blew in from the North. So, instead of refueling the lantern, he waited patiently for the Elizabeth Dame's lights to glimmer on the inland sea, knowing the Captain would be relying on the flashing beacon of the Twin Rock Lighthouse to steer him and his crew away from danger."

"How did he know which lights would be the Elizabeth Dame?" Little Jimmy asked.

"Ya, another good question." The tour guide raised his left brow, and added. "Having been the keeper for a long time, William Young knew the route and schedule of each passing ship. But he didn't have to be the keeper to know the schedule of the Elizabeth Dame because, you see, its Captain was his brother."

Little Jimmy scratched his head. "But how did he know for sure which lights were the Elizabeth Dame?"

"Ya, right. Like I told ya folks in the beginning, William Young waited and watched through the north port window." The crowd turned in the direction of his pointing hand. "After the foghorn blared at midnight he spotted a faint light in the distance and, as always, his brother flashed the signal light of the Elizabeth Dame three times. Then William Young slowly burned out the lantern's flame and stood quietly in the darkness of the roaring waves, waiting for the Elizabeth Dame to smash into smithereens against the cliffs." The crowd gasped.

"But the story doesn't end there, folks. Once he made sure his brother was out of the way, William Young descended the spiral staircase and, like he did every night after his keeper duties, headed back to the cabin to join his sleeping wife. Only that night he didn't intend on sleeping. That night he intended on hacking his wife up into tiny little pieces."

"Why did he do it? Didn't he love them?" An elderly woman asked.

"You betcha he did. You see it was no secret to the folks in town that William Young's brother was having an affair with his wife. Only thing was the last person in town to find out was William. It's said he went crazy with jealousy."

The elderly woman clutched her purse. "What happened to him, the keeper?"

"Well, after he had carried out his plan, William Young walked to the edge of the cliffs and threw himself into the raging water, joining his brother and the crew of the Elizabeth Dame in their watery graves. By the way, the Elizabeth Dame was named for his wife." The crowd took turns peering through the port window overlooking the cliffs.

The tour guide knocked against the metal post of the lantern. "Every so often a ship will report seeing a shining beacon coming from the Twin Rock Lighthouse."

"But, I thought you said this isn't a lighthouse anymore?" Little Jimmy asked.

"You betcha I did!" The tour guide raised his left brow. "Legend has it he still roams the grounds reliving that night over and over."

The crowd descended the spiral staircase, following behind the silent footsteps of William Young.

* * * *

William Young stomped across the frozen lawn to the toolshed and grabbed an axe. Inch by inch, he opened the door he promised Elizabeth he'd oil back in September and made his way through the darkened cabin. Frozen tears clung to his beard as he swung the axe high above his head and hacked his beloved wife to death, again.

Flash Five – Spying on the Dead
Based on the theme: Mortuaries

It wasn't easy growing up in a town where everybody knew everybody, and everybody associated your name with death.

You see, my father was the town's only mortician and, sooner or later, people knew they would eventually pass through our house on their way to the other side. I'm sure that's why no one living ever came to visit my parents or why I never had any friends come to play with me. With the exception of Eddie and Sue.

Some of my fondest memories from childhood are the ones of the three of us playing hide and seek or red light, green light. Our summers were never spent apart, not even the summer Sue died.

Ever since the second grade, when Eddie and I first asked Sue if we could sit with her at lunch, her beauty captivated me. I can still recall the sparkle in her eyes that were the color of a golden pond and her long silken hair that was the color of night, and the way she'd fling it behind her shoulders, as if she were Queen of the Nile, and give us her Mona Lisa smile. Even though Eddie ended up winning her affection I never stopped loving her.

As the years flew by, playing hide and seek and red light, green light became passé, and so, during the summer between ninth and tenth grade the three of us looked for new ways to fill the long hot days. That's when Eddie came up with the idea to play a game; he dubbed, spying on the dead.

Eddie's plan was to wait until my father got a call to pick up a dead person from the morgue and then the three of us would sneak inside the mortuary and hide and spy. At first, Sue was hesitant to play the game because she was afraid my mother would catch us, but I reassured her the only way my mother would step inside the mortuary was if she were dead.

21

And so, that summer, we waited and waited for someone to die. Looking back, I wish the first time we played spying on the dead that Sue's fears had come true and we had been caught…

* * * *

Eddie threw the dice, picked up his game piece and moved it five spaces. The phone rang and the three of us paused, and waited.

The click clack of my mother's heels followed her down the hall. "Taylor's Mortuary. Yes, I'll let him know." She hung up the receiver. "David, your patient is ready at the morgue!"

Eddie smiled.

Sue giggled. "Patient?"

I rolled my eyes, and shrugged. "She doesn't like to think of them as dead people."

My father trotted down the stairs, my heart pounding with his every step. I picked up the dice and rolled. "Come on, let's keep playing until it's safe."

The crackling and crunching of the graveled driveway faded to silence. "Mother! We're going to go outside and bum around, okay?"

"Alright, Steven. You three have fun!"

We raced each other to the overgrown shrubs that hid the view of the mortuary from the house. I held open a small opening in the middle and motioned for Eddie to go first. Sue grabbed his hand and followed him through. I checked again to be sure my mother wasn't watching and disappeared into the shrubs.

Eddie bent down to tie his loosened shoestring. "Steven, how are we going to get in? Doesn't your dad keep the doors locked?"

I reached down into a pile of rocks, used as landscaping, and picked up the only gray one. I turned it over and waived my hand back and forth. "Abracadabra!" I spun the key high above my head.

Eddie smiled. "Very clever."

Sue followed Eddie and I down the long corridor, her sneakers squeaking across the waxed floor. "Guys, where are we going?"

I paused, and turned. "Mwah! The embalming room."

Sue twirled the strand of hair wrapped around her finger, twice. "Quit teasing me like that!"

"Who said I was teasing?"

"I think maybe this wasn't such a good idea." She turned to walk away.

Eddie grabbed her by the hand. "Oh, come on, Sue. This is going to be really cool."

"I . . . I don't know."

Eddie sighed. "Will you do it for a kiss?"

She looked at me, and gave her Mona Lisa smile. "Okay."

I knew the perfect place to hide would be inside the closet my father used to store all the dirty magazines he didn't want my mother to know he had. I led the way past the embalming table, cleaned and ready for its next arrival, and opened the closet door.

Sue squealed. "Oh my gosh, Steven. What's this scary looking prong used for?" She lifted it with two fingers.

"That's a trocar and trust me you only want that shoved into your organs when you're dead."

Eddie grabbed it out of her hand. "I told you this was going to be really cool!"

The corridor filled with the sudden screeching of squeaky wheels. "It's my father!" I motioned for them to hurry.

Eddie returned the trocar and led Sue by the hand into the closet.

"Would you look at all these magazines?" He picked one from the pile. "Wow, now that's what I call a pair!" Sue snatched it from his grip and slapped it across his shoulder.

"Shhh! Be quite you two, he's almost here." The anticipation of what was to come rose from my stomach and into my throat.

Huddled together, we peered through the slats of the door and waited. My father wheeled the body bag next to the embalming table and slowly slid open the zipper, exposing our first spying on the dead corpse. "Hello, Henry, and how are you today?" Unable to answer, Mr. Zimmer, the town librarian, stared up at my father.

Sue gasped and hid her face in Eddie's shirt.

"You're dad talks to dead people?" Eddie whispered.

I responded with a flick of my finger to his ear.

My father pushed the play button on the cassette player and slowly waved his hands in the air. He picked up a pair of gloves and shoved his hands inside, snapping the rubber against his wrist. After hooking Mr. Zimmer up to the pulley, my father flipped the switch and continued conducting his violin music.

Mr. Zimmer's naked body rose into the air and glided toward the embalming table. Sue whimpered and I quickly cupped my hand over her mouth. My father paused, turned off the cassette player and pulley, and glanced around the room. Shrugging, he restarted the pulley and helped guide naked Mr. Zimmer down onto the table.

My father picked up the trocar, turned on the suction, and shoved it into Mr. Zimmer's stomach. Sue whimpered in my cupped hand, sending a quiver up my arm and down my leg. It was the first time, and the last time, she ever did that to me . . . alive.

* * * *

We spent two hours that day inside the closet watching my father prepare Mr. Zimmer for his journey to the other side. But it wouldn't be the last time that summer we played spying on the dead. There was Mrs. Daniels from church, Mr. Terwilliger from the gas station and Mr. Hooper from the bank.

It was after then Eddie wanted to place a bet on who in town was going to be the next corpse. For the fun of it I bet on him, and in return, he bet on me. That's when Sue came up with the idea of playing a joke on my father. She would be the next corpse.

At first I didn't like the idea, but Sue convinced me to go along with her prank in exchange for a kiss. Looking back, I wish I never had wanted to kiss her…

* * * *

After my father's van disappeared out of sight I picked up the receiver and dialed. "Hey, Eddie, my parents just left to go into town. I'll meet you and Sue in fifteen minutes in front of the mortuary."

I searched for a piece of paper and pen and read aloud as I wrote down the phony message. "Father, the morgue came by while you were gone. They had a patient to deliver so I let them in. They said they'd call later with the details. Steven."

I pushed through the shrubs and took the key out of the rock. Sue ran ahead of Eddie. "I'm so excited!" She paused to catch her breath.

"We better hurry, they won't be gone very long." I unlocked the door and returned the key to its hiding place.

Eddie and I followed Sue and her squeaking sneakers down the corridor to the embalming room. She turned. "You two wait out here while I get ready. I'll let you know when you can come in." She flung her hair behind her shoulders, and gave us her Mona Lisa smile.

I tapped my foot again and re-checked the corridor. "She better hurry up, my father could be here any minute."

Eddie knocked on the door. "Sue, are you ready?"

"Okay, you can come in now!"

Sue lay on top of the embalming table, covered by a sheet. Eddie lifted its ends, and paused. "I wonder who our patient is today?"

"Eddie, no! I want everything to be a surprise."

The corridor filled with whistling. "My father! Hurry, Eddie, let's hide."

Shoving our way inside the closet, Eddie tripped over something on the floor. "Wow, Steven, Sue doesn't have any clothes on!"

"Shhh, be quite, he's almost here." My stomach fluttered at the thought of her on the table, cold and naked.

We stood shoulder to shoulder, peering through the slats in the door. My father started his violin music, slapped rubber gloves over his hands and waved them high in the air. "Well, who do we have today?" He pulled back the sheet, and gasped.

Eddie and I cupped our hands over our mouths, and whimpered. Sue lay stiff as a board on her back with her arms tucked tightly against her body, her breast picture perfect like the magazines that surrounded us.

My father turned and clanked several tools on top of a silver tray. "It's never easy when they're so young." Sue looked back at us and smiled, skipping my thumping heart.

Without hesitating, my father spun around and drove a scalpel straight into Sue's jugular. And, just like Mrs. Daniels and Mr. Hooper's' dead bodies had done, Sue bolted straight up. Only she was able to scream.

＊ ＊ ＊ ＊

Even in death Sue's long silken hair, the color of night, and her Mona Lisa smile captivated me. I'll remember my good-bye kiss to her, forever.

Flash Six – Night of the Senior Prom
Based on the theme: Dance of the Dead or Undead

The sun crept through the torn sheets Granny used as a sorry excuse for drapes and I smiled for the first time in months. Ever since Mama and I moved to this dead-beat town six months ago to live with her I haven't felt human. But, yesterday, my crappy existence changed.

"When the sunbeam gets to the large crack in the middle of the ceiling I'm gonna get up." I promised myself aloud. Stretching my thick legs over the end of the same bed I've had since I was twelve, I thought about health class yesterday and how dorky Mr. Burns looked explaining how the sperm found its perfect mate.

I chuckled. "Hum, I wonder what Brad Westlake is doing right now?" I guess Mama's right when she preaches about how anyone's life can change in a day. I'm sure it's not every day that someone like Brad, an all star senior quarterback, and just about the hottest guy at Valley Hill High, asks an all star nobody from out of town to the Senior Prom. I can't wait to see the look on the cheerleading squad's starving wannabe supermodel faces when he walks into the dance holding hands with a well fed, never worn lip gloss, nail polish or eyeliner super bitch!

Holding true to my promise, I got out of bed and pulled a pair of stretchy jeans and a faded tee shirt from the dirty clothes pile. Giving some thought to how my frizzy hair looked for the first time since maybe sixth grade I walked into the bathroom and confirmed it looked best in a ponytail, like it does every day.

I flipped on the hallway switch and the light bulb popped. "Ugh! How long am I going to have to live in this hell hole?" Yawning my way down the darkened hallway and into the kitchen I joined Mama and Granny at the table. "Morning." I shoveled a forkful of the triple stacked pancakes in my mouth, dripping butter and syrup down my chin.

Mama looked up from her spread out newspaper. "Morning, Tracey Ann."

Granny nodded and smiled.

Mama closed the paper and folded it in half. "I just read that Valley Hill High's Senior Prom is this weekend. Be nice if you were going."

I shoveled in another forkful. "I am."

Mama jumped up and lifted Granny by the arm and the two burst into a silent square dance.

"Oh, Mama, it's nothing special. He's just some boy from the football team."

She stopped and staggered over to me and patted me on the head. "Tracey Ann, going to your Senior Prom is a very big deal. It's a dance you'll remember for the rest of your life."

✳ ✳ ✳ ✳

The week went as slow as sap dripping from a tree in winter, but finally Saturday arrived. I couldn't wait for six o'clock to come and for my hunk of a date to roar into the driveway in his mustang that's blacker than Mama's burnt bacon on Sunday's.

I opened and turned the tube of cherry red lipstick I snatched from Mama's purse and glided it around my lips and puckered. The light over the bathroom mirror flickered. "That doesn't look so bad." I ran a brush over my sorry attempt at curling frizzy hair, and sighed. "It will have to do."

The purple prom dress I found at Retro Dresses and More rustled as I made my way down the hallway and into the living room. Mama sat laughing at the same stupid episodes of I Love Lucy she watched every Saturday night and Granny sat knitting the most hideous blanket I'd ever seen. "Is that for me, Granny?"

Ignoring me, she nodded.

I twirled, clearing my throat. "How do I look?"

Mama mimicked a line with Ethel and looked up. "Tracey Ann, you'll knock 'em all dead."

"Granny, what do you think?"

She replied with a nod.

I pulled the drape aside and pushed down the blind for the umpteenth time. The empty driveway had turned dark. "Mama, I think my date forgot to pick me up. I'm gonna walk down to the school."

Mama chuckled and slapped her hand across her knee. "That gets me every time."

I grabbed the beaded handbag Mama said she took to her school dance and swung open the front door. "Good night, don't wait up."

"Tracey Ann?"

"Yes, Granny?"

She wrapped a piece of brown yarn twice around the knitting needle. "I'd be careful if I were you. Things ain't been right in this town ever since them kids started changing." She paused. "Oh, I can never remember what they call them." Shrugging, she weaved the yarn into my hideous blanket.

"Sure, Granny, I will." Geez, when she does talk she says the weirdest things.

* * * *

The clacking of the only worn out high-heeled shoes I could find, that even the tallest guy on the basketball team could wear, followed me down the sidewalk like a parrot. Checking left, then right, I stepped off the curb and crossed the street. "That's strange, where is everybody?"

Turning the corner, every window of Valley Hill High flashed like the disco floor from that old movie Mama talked me into watching on her birthday last year. "Geez, you could wake the dead with that music!"

Pulling open the main doors, the music and lights disappeared. "Brad?" My voice echoed through the darkness. "I know you all are in here!" Determined not to let them get away with their stupid prank I propped open the doors, and using my hands, followed the lockers down the hall and around the corner to the gymnasium.

Pausing to adjust my bra and panties, I took a deep breath and pushed my way through the doors. Silhouetted shadows blocked the only light source from the emergency exit signs. "What the hell is going on?"

A darkened figure stepped forward. "Tracey Ann, I'm glad you made it."

"Why in the hell didn't you pick me up and what's with the stupid prank?"

"What prank?" The gymnasium lights blasted on.

Blinded, I used my hands as a shield. "What happened? You look like you stuck your face in a meat grinder."

Brad grinned. "Nothing happened. You just haven't seen me without my mask."

One by one the football team, followed by the cheerleading squad and the rest of the dead-beat school, ripped off their faces. "Now's a fine time for Granny to finally make sense." I turned to run toward the door.

Brad grabbed hold of my arm and pulled me close to him. "It's mandatory for all teenage zombies to wear one." He pressed his all star rotting lips against Mama's cherry red lipstick and sunk his teeth into my bottom lip, tearing it from my all star nobody face.

Mama was right. My Senior Prom is a dance I'll remember for the rest of my crappy, endless, life.

Bonus Flash! – Behind the Cellar Door
Based on the theme: Dark Spaces

Growing up in the middle of somewhere between miles of unpaved roads and abundant cornfields never bothered Jayden Mitchell. She knew her foster parents, Missy and Henry, had given her a life far better than any orphanage.

Soon to be eighteen, Jayden had been eagerly waiting to live out her dreams. For as far back as she could remember they had all been the same; turn eighteen, marry her high school sweetheart, move into a farmhouse, raise lots of children and live happily ever after.

All that changed two months ago, when her blissful dreams suddenly turned dark and sinister.

* * * *

Running nowhere from the surrounding suffocation of faceless shadows Jayden turned the enormous doorknob with both hands, melting it in her heated clutch. Realizing the doom of her fate Jayden silently screamed out into the fading light, scratching and clawing her way through the endless door.

Bam! Bam! Bam!

Jayden's screams grew louder and louder with every screeching claw mark she made against the splintering wood.

Bam! Bam! Bam!

The distant voice increasingly becoming familiar to Jayden awakened her senses. "Missy?

"Jayden, you better be up and getting ready. If you're not downstairs in ten minutes we'll miss the noon bus into town. I will not tolerate us missing our appointment!"

Grabbing the end of her overused pillow, Jayden turned onto her right side and stuffed it over her head.

"Jayden Mitchell, you get your ass up or you'll be confined to your room until I see fit!"

"Okay, Mother. I'll be down in five!" Missy's footsteps faded into distant echoes.

Jayden sat up and grabbed her cell phone off the nightstand. "Someone's forgotten I turn eighteen in two days." She pulled up Tate Brandon's image and with no time to waste typed out her message...I so cannot wait until my birthday on Friday and our secret escape. I love you with all my heart. Your soon to be wife, Jay D.

* * * *

The bus roared down the dry sandstone road known to the local kids as the highway to nowhere. They knew beyond the town's non-existent borders there was no freedom awaiting them. Only outsiders dreamed of such a thing.

Countless rows of corn ready for harvesting flashed by Jayden's limited view through the neglected bus window, turning her attention to the last two months. The only explanation she could think of as to why, after all these years, her foster parents began treating her so rotten was they wanted her to leave.

Jayden surrendered to the nagging urge to come clean on her secret. "Missy..." She paused, at the slip of her tongue. "Mother?"

Without looking up from scribbling in her notebook, Missy replied. "What is it? The bus squealed to a grinding halt.

"Um, where are we going?"

Shoving the notebook into her overflowing handbag, Missy was the first to stand. "Hurry, we don't want to be late."

Stepping off the bus, the mixture of diesel fuel, fried onions and overcooked burgers from Harvey's on the corner made Jayden regret her only source of breakfast was a half-eaten candy bar left over from yesterday.

Leading the way, Missy swung open the county clinic's door and motioned for Jayden to go inside. "You mustn't keep the doctor waiting."

Jayden froze. "Why do I have to see the doctor? I'm not sick."

"Because it's time."

"Time for what?"

"Get inside, Jayden, or I will drag you in by your hair if I have to."

Holding back her breakfast with a burning backwash of chocolate and caramel, Jayden rushed past the empty waiting room and straight into the ladies room.

* * * *

The vibration of the bus engine failed to silence the whimpering voice inside Jayden's head. "How could she let that creepy Dr. Higgins violate me like that? Tate was supposed to be the first one ever to see and touch my private sanctum, not some old balding fat guy."

Missy caressed the back of her hand down Jayden's face, smearing mascara across her cheeks. "You're going to be an adult in a few days. We just needed to be sure."

Jayden turned her head and numbly watched the blurring cornfields, imagining what the freedom that awaited her on the other side looked like.

* * * *

With the anticipation of her escape, Jayden awoke Friday morning alert and full of energy. Finally, for the first time in weeks, she had dreamt of farmhouses, children and living happily ever after. She smiled knowing her nightmares were over.

Jayden rolled over and grabbed her cell phone off the nightstand and tapped speed dial number two. "Good morning, husband to be." She whispered after the first ring. "I'm…"

"Happy Birthday!" Tate interrupted.

"Thanks, I'm so excited. I'm finally 18!"

"Do your parents suspect anything?"

"I don't think so." She paused, listening for an intruding ear pressed against the bedroom door. "They said they didn't make any plans, because they have an important meeting in town and they weren't sure what time they'd be home."

Tate howled. "Don't forget, baby. I'll meet you tonight at eight thirty sharp at the old abandoned church on Route 19."

"There's no way I'd forget. I've been dreaming of this day for as long as I can remember."

"Oh, and Mrs. Brandon?"

She snickered. "Yes, Mr. Brandon?"

"Don't be late."

"Believe me, I wouldn't be late if my life depended on it."

* * * *

The clock on the mantel chimed twice. "I thought you and Dad had an important meeting in town?" Jayden tapped her right foot against the wooden floor.

Missy sat knitting a pink and white blanket. "We do. It was moved back a couple of hours." She glanced at the clock. "It's almost time."

Before the tell tale signs of the truck's overdue maintenance had faded away, Jayden began scrambling to pack the small suitcase she found tucked in the attic behind stacks and stacks of faded newspapers and envelopes.

Jayden sat on the couch with her hands clasped together, praying for the absence of headlights against the darkening walls. When the encroaching night devoured the last remnants of the sun she knew freedom was within in her grasp. She opened her overstuffed suitcase and stared at the handwritten envelope. "It's now or never, Jayden." She slammed the lid shut, clicked the locks and placed the sealed letter on top of Missy's knitting bag; in hopes they would one-day come to forgive her.

The mantel clock struck its eighth chime as Jayden swung open the front door. She turned for one last glance at the only home she'd ever known, and smiled. "It's, finally, time."

* * * *

The harvest moon illuminated against the starless sky like a beacon of hope to Jayden. She paused and swallowed a mouthful of the cool still night before shoving her way inside the thickened cornfield, ignoring Tate's advice. She knew the main road was the fastest, and safest, way to the church, but she'd rather take a chance on getting lost in a maze of corn than being caught running away.

Time became non-existent to Jayden as she wandered deeper through the towering cornstalks. Singing katydids stole any chances of listening for life outside the entangling maze. Jayden set the suitcase on the ground and pulled her cell phone from her back pocket. "God, please let there be a sign." The phone screen blank, she plopped down on the ground and prayed.

A soft breeze swept through the surrounding wall of corn and across her face, revealing a glimmer of hope in the distance. "Thank you, God!"

Making her way toward the light, Jayden refused to let the over-powering force of the field keep her from carrying out her plan.

* * * *

Jayden shoved her way past the remaining fortress of corn, tripping on a vine that had long ago invaded the abandoned church grounds. Unable to catch her fall, she landed hands and knees on top of her scattered clothes.

She stood and brushed herself clean, spotting the pitiful excuse of a wedding dress she bought at a thrift store for less than the cost of a movie and a small bag of popcorn on matinee Sunday's. "Oh no!" She raised it into the moonlight. Imprints of dirt and grass stains covered the time worn dress. "Damn it." She gathered her once neatly folded panties, bras and runaway clothes and repacked them, flinging her useless wedding dress on top and shoving the lid closed.

The crunching of footsteps joined in with the singing katydids. "Tate, I'm over here!"

The katydids replied . . . in silence.

Jayden stood and searched through the blue haze of the cascading moonlight. "Tate, is that you?"

"Over here, Jayden."

Relieved, Jayden spun toward his echoing voice. The church stood like a decrepit giant weeping in the night. "Where? I don't see you."

"I'm inside waiting for you."

* * * *

Jayden pushed her way past the half-hinged door and stepped inside the moonlit church. Rows of rotted pews stood silent in the stagnant air and overgrown vines covered the walls like slithering snakes in search of food. "Tate?" Without warning, a violent rancid wind swept through the room and slammed the rickety door shut, leaving Jayden alone in the dark. "Please, you're beginning to scare me."

"I'm here, Jayden. Just follow the light."

She opened her eyes as wide as they could. A dim light flickered from behind the altar. "Why are you hiding from me?"

"I'm not hiding. I have a surprise for our special night."

Jayden pulled the battered luggage tight against her chest and made her way toward the flickering light. Placing her only worldly possessions at the foot of the altar she walked around it one step at a time and bent over the opened storm cellar. "Tate, please, this isn't very funny."

"Seriously, Jayden, I have a surprise for you. Hurry on down."

The surrounding stoned walls seemed to swallow the winding wooden staircase as Jayden descended into the damp cellar. "Your surprise better be worth all this." She stepped off the last step, and gasped.

Tate stood behind an altar, lit by rows and rows of candles, dressed in a black robe from head to toe. He pointed to a table with a neatly laid out wedding gown, and smiled.

Jayden clutched at her heart. "I don't understand."

Bam! Clunk! Footsteps echoed down the stairway.

Jayden spun in a circle. "Who's there?"

Tate stepped down from the altar. "Don't be afraid. You're very special to me."

"You are very special to us, too." Missy and Henry stood at the foot of the stairs.

The darkness of the walls became alive with faceless shadows. "And, to the whole town."

Realizing her nightmares were about to come true, Jayden Mitchell ran nowhere from the surrounding suffocation of faceless shadows she had once called friends, scratching and clawing into the fading light.

* * * *

Missy Mitchell spread the pink and white knit blanket across the bed and laid the infant on top. "Oh, Henry, isn't she just beautiful."

Henry finished reading the paper's headline . . . Authorities clueless on whereabouts of kidnapped newborn.

"Henry, don't you think our new daughter is beautiful?"

"Yes, of course, I do." He closed the paper. "But, what's really beautiful is another 18 years of abundant crops."

The End

ABOUT THE AUTHOR

T.K. Millin lives along Florida's West Coast, known as the Nature Coast, along with her husband and their feline family members. One of which is the infamous black sagacious feline, Efi Loo, The Cat Vamp.

It wasn't until after T.K. Millin began her writing career that she discovered she had a very talented ghostwriter waiting to be discovered. Each of the stories featured in Fiction in a Flash! were co-authored by Efi Loo. T.K. Millin is a member of Mystery Writers of America and Society of Children's Books Writers & Illustrators.

T.K. Millin's short story, Mr. Jingle, can be found in the anthology, Satan's Toybox: Demonic Dolls, published in 2011 by Angelic Knight Press. Her first children's short story, Shells For Hunter; part of her series, Bedtime Stories on the Go, was published by Efi Loo Publishing in 2012 as an EBook.

When not writing, T.K. Millin can be found gardening, rescuing and finding a forever home for the occasional stray that wanders into her garden and, well, writing. Efi Loo? Let's just say, keep the tuna handy and watch your fingers, because Cat Vamp's love to bite!

COMING SOON!

BACK IN A FLASH!
SEVEN TALES THAT SCARE

Based on all new flash fiction shorts

By

T.K. Millin

www.ingramcontent.com/pod-product-compliance
Lightning Source LLC
Chambersburg PA
CBHW071222130626
46555CB00004B/1799